THE STORM

AMERICAN CHAPTERS

GRETA GORSUCH

WAYZGOOSE PRESS

Book design and editing by Maggie Sokolik, Wayzgoose Press

Cover design by DJ Rogers, Book Branders

CONTENTS

FROM THE AUTHOR

Welcome to our series, *American Chapters*. The *American Chapters* series presents short stories in vivid and easy-to-read 500-word chapters, perfect for English language learners internationally, and adult literacy learners in countries where English is commonly used.

All *American Chapters* stories are also offered as audiobooks, narrated by the author, for learners who want to read the stories and hear the sounds of American English.

American Chapters are lively, relevant, and realistic short stories about living in the United States of America. About Americans, immigrants, sojourners, and the diverse peoples living in this wide landscape, the stories touch on the tough questions, and the great things in life—things like work, ethnic differences, our connections to the past, our place in nature, being new, small town life, personal loss, and above all, new beginnings.

CHAPTER ONE

Cecilia woke up before the alarm clock went off. The alarm was set for 6 AM, but she was out of bed at 5:45. She felt good. She went to bed early the night before. She slept well. She was ready for the day ahead.

It was getting light in the east. The sun would rise soon.

There was enough light for Cecilia to see her back yard stretch off into the distance. The only other thing she could see were her three white wind turbines. Their long white blades were busy this morning. They moved quickly in the dark, cool air, going *whish whish whish*. The Windspeed turbines made electricity for her house. Cecilia had not paid for electricity in three years.

Cecilia felt a little pulse of happiness. All that space, and only grass and wind in it. Cecilia lived in the country. There was a lot of open land around her house. She lived in West Texas, after all. It had only a few small towns, and they were far apart. She could drive twenty miles before she saw a town ahead, way off in the distance. Five more miles of driving might bring her a little closer to the town, although not much. Cecilia's closest neighbor was a ten-minute drive away. It was an hour on foot if your car wouldn't start.

It was already October. The terrible heat of the Texas summer was fading away. This morning, before the sun came up, it was cool. Early morning made Cecilia think of colors, like cool blues and purples and silvers. This was how the morning sky looked.

Cecilia's taste in clothes was different. Usually she liked to wear pinks, oranges, and reds. She sometimes wore red shoes and pink socks together. Cecilia liked having nice fingernails and hair.

One of her clients, Mrs. Gold, was used to seeing Cecilia wear all sorts of colors. One morning, Cecilia wore orange fingernail polish to match her new orange "I Take Care of It" work t-shirt. She wore an orange ribbon in her long dark hair. Mrs. Gold, seeing the triple orange combination, sat stunned in her easy chair. Her mouth opened, but she didn't say anything.

Cecilia handed Mrs. Gold a cold drink of water. Cecilia found that was a good way to help people get over something they were not expecting. The glass of water worked.

After a few minutes, Mrs. Gold said, "My goodness Cecilia, that's a bright fingernail polish you're wearing."

"Yep, it's pretty bright," Cecilia said, moving around and sweeping Mrs. Gold's floor.

It was 6:30 in the morning. Cecilia looked out at the sun coming up. She thought about what she wanted to wear. She had three houses to visit for her "I Take Care of It" business. The visits would take until 2 PM. She could wear jeans and her orange "I Take Care of It" t-shirt for that. Then, she had some banking business in Sunflower. She might have enough time to drive home to get something to eat. She needed to change her clothes for her night class in Lubbock. Class was at 6 PM. Lubbock was the largest town in the area. It was a ninety minute drive away. She couldn't leave her house any later than 4 PM. Time would be tight.

For her night class, Cecilia wore different clothes. Somehow, her oranges and reds and pinks didn't fit in. When she thought of the night class on home care for the elderly, she got the same image she got from early mornings in her back yard: Cool blues, purples, and silvers. Cecilia decided what to wear that night. She took out some dark slacks and a purple shirt and laid them on her bed for later. It was time to get started on the long day ahead of her.

CHAPTER TWO

Cecilia's orange "I Take Care of It" t-shirts were a sign of a big change in her life. Just four months earlier, Cecilia owned a house cleaning business. She wore pink "I Clean It" t-shirts then. "I Clean It" was the name of the business she had with her partner, Frannie Clifton. Frannie died. It was a huge shock. Even worse, Cecilia then learned that Frannie cheated Cecilia and their clients out of money. Before she died, Frannie became a gambling addict. She used her laptop computer to gamble on websites. She used the money she stole from their clients.

The idea of Frannie taking money that wasn't theirs was like looking into a deep black hole. Cecilia couldn't understand it. She still wasn't over it.

All of this made Cecilia think about things. She saw her life in new ways. In her "I Clean It" business, she cleaned houses for anyone who paid her. Some of her clients were single and Cecilia's age—in their thirties. They drove to Plainview or Lubbock to work. Some of her clients were families with children in school.

Her other clients were old men and women. They were the elderly citizens of the town. They didn't get out very much. They had money from farming or ranching. They needed their houses cleaned, just as Cecilia's younger clients did. But the older folks needed extra help with day-to-day things. Things people don't usually think of if they are young.

They needed Cecilia to do laundry, pay bills, look through their mail, and check their bank accounts. They couldn't drive, so they needed Cecilia to drive them to Plainview to see the doctor, or go to the shopping center to buy clothes. Sunflower didn't have a doctor or a shopping center.

Cecilia's first home visit this morning was to Mrs. Gold. Mrs. Gold had a small white house on 6th Street in Sunflower. All of the houses on 6th Street were built in the 1920s. Some of the houses looked good. Others were empty and forgotten-looking. The "good" houses had fresh paint and nice yards. In West Texas, where it was so dry, people watered the lawn only once a week. If they had trees, they watered them, too.

This morning, Cecilia pulled out Mrs. Gold's water hose. She put the end of it at the base of Mrs. Gold's big tree in the front yard. She turned on the water, but just a little. A thin trickle of water spilled out to go deep into the tree's roots.

Cecilia went into the house. "Good morning Mrs. Gold!" she called out.

"Is that you Cecilia?" Mrs. Gold asked. As usual, she was in the bathroom. If Mrs. Gold was having a bad day, she stayed in the bathroom. She was sensitive about her hair. Mrs. Gold used regular bath soap to wash her hair. No wonder she had so much trouble with it. Cecilia got Mrs. Gold some nice shampoo to help.

Whether or not Mrs. Gold was having a bad day, Cecilia made sure she came out of the bathroom at least once. She knocked on the bathroom door. "Yes, Mrs. Gold, it's me," Cecilia said. "Are you OK in there?" She went to check Mrs. Gold's refrigerator. Today was grocery store day for Mrs. Gold.

"I'm comin', I'm comin'!" Mrs. Gold said. In a few minutes, she came out of the bathroom. She was wearing regular clothes. Her short curly gray hair looked OK. Cecilia took her for a haircut last week. She had on blue slacks and a white flowered shirt. This was unusual. Mrs. Gold almost always wore a nightgown.

"I'm comin' with you to the grocery store," Mrs. Gold said.

Cecilia laughed. This was a good thing. Mrs. Gold almost never left the house.

"OK," Cecilia said. "But remember, I have to be done by 9:30 this morning. I have to go over to Mr. Harrison's place before lunch."

"All right. You're always in a hurry!" Mrs. Gold said.

CHAPTER THREE

Cecilia gave Mrs. Gold the grocery list. She made sure Mrs. Gold had her seatbelt on.

"My, it sure is bright," Mrs. Gold said. She put her thin, pale hand over her eyes against the sun. It was a bright morning. It would get warm today.

They drove to the Sunflower Pay Day Supermarket. It was one of the three big stores in town that was still open. Sunflower also had a Nabor's Drug Store, and a Family Dollar store.

The parking lot at the Pay Day Supermarket was half full. Cecilia got Mrs. Gold a shopping cart. Mrs. Gold pushed the cart. It helped her walk. A few customers called out to Mrs. Gold. "Essie!" one middle-aged woman said. "I haven't seen you for ages!"

Mrs. Gold called out to an older man, "Hi Davey! It's been awhile!" The elderly man waved back. It was a good thing Essie Gold was out of the house today.

Cecilia looked at her watch. They needed to keep moving if

she was going to keep to her schedule. She still had two more houses to visit before two o'clock.

Mrs. Gold's grocery list included oranges and lemons. The store had lemons, but no oranges.

"What do you need the oranges for?" Cecilia asked. "Can we get something else? How about some apples?"

"Oh, I just wanted some fresh orange juice," Mrs. Gold said. "I had some once on my honeymoon in Florida."

"When was that?" Cecilia asked. In her night class on home healthcare, she learned it was important to ask old people to talk about dates and memories.

"Sixty-two years ago!" Mrs. Gold laughed. "Think that's a long time ago?"

"A bit," Cecilia said. "Well, maybe we can get some frozen orange juice. How about that?"

They went slowly over to the frozen food section and got a few cans of frozen orange juice. Cecilia would make some for Mrs. Gold before she left.

On the way out of the grocery store, Cecilia picked up a copy of the *Sunflower Reporter*, a newspaper that came out once a week. She gave it to Mrs. Gold to read on the way home. They drove to Mrs. Gold's little house.

Mrs. Gold said, "It says here that a new café is opening up."

"Oh?" Cecilia said. "I think I know the building. It's right over there." She slowed down and pointed at the old Grandview News and Soda Shop. It had gone out of business twenty years ago. It was still empty.

Cecilia and Essie Gold saw a sign in the window:

COMING SOON!
LINDA'S CAFÉ AND LUNCH SPOT

Cecilia saw two workers inside. They were painting the walls a creamy white.

"Hmmm," Mrs. Gold said.

As they drove down 6th Street, they saw something else. The big old Garcia house on the corner had a car and a work truck in front of it. The front door was open. Cecilia stopped her car.

"Well," Mrs. Gold said, with her little Texas twang.

The Garcia house was one of the empty, forgotten houses on 6th Street. It was a beautiful stone house with two stories and a steep 1920s-style roof. After Mr. and Mrs. Garcia died in 1970, their children moved away.

Cecilia was just a small child then, but she remembered it. By the time Cecilia was in high school, the windows on the house were all broken. The front lawn was brown and dead from the dry Texas summers, with no one to water it.

Cecilia drove Mrs. Gold to her house. She carried in the bags of groceries and put them away. She made some orange juice. She reminded Mrs. Gold she would come again on Thursday. They needed to drive to Plainview to see the doctor.

"OK," Mrs. Gold said. "Bye, Cecilia!"

"See you!" Cecilia said.

Then she drove away.

CHAPTER FOUR

Cecilia visited two more clients. Mr. Harrison lived in a big farmhouse between Sunflower and the town of Lockney. He needed cleaning and laundry done. Lately, though, his handwriting had gotten bad. He also needed help writing checks to pay his bills.

"After fifty years of driving trucks and tractors, I guess my right hand wants to take a vacation!" he said. He held up his large, hard hand. It shook from age.

Mr. Harrison was 87. His wife had died five years before. Cecilia sat down with Mr. Harrison at the kitchen table. She wrote out checks for him. One check was for the electricity bill. Another was for health insurance. Mr. Harrison also had some large deposits for the bank. He had oil on his land. He got money from the oil company every month.

He said, "I've been contacted by a wind electrical power company."

"Oh?" Cecilia said.

"They want to put wind turbines on my land, west of here," he said. "They can pay me something each year. You know how strong the wind is in these parts. They can make a lot of electricity from those turbines. I might make a lot of money."

"What do you think about that?" Cecilia asked. "Is there any down side? Can you think of anything wrong with it?"

"I don't know yet," Mr. Harrison said. "I'm still thinking about it. They seem awfully eager, though. They called me twice last week! They called again just before you got here. That makes me think I should wait a bit more."

They laughed together. He gave Cecilia the things she needed for his banking in Sunflower.

Mr. Harrison's youngest son, Hack Harrison, had contacted Cecilia two months before. Hack and Cecilia were old friends. They went to high school together. Hack and his family lived in Dallas, so he needed someone to visit his father twice a week.

"Dad told me what you were doing. You know, working with the elderly," Hack said. "Dad talks about your father all the time, you know. He really liked your father."

"I'm glad to hear that," Cecilia said. She was quiet for a minute. She missed her father. Her father, Clarence Hunter of Sunflower, was a farmer, just like Mr. Harrison. Then she said, "Anyway, I'm happy to help. When do you want me to start?"

"Are you bonded?" Hack Harrison asked.

"Yes, I am," Cecilia said. "I can mail you my bond paperwork today, if you like." She mailed it. Cecilia started her visits to old Mr. Harrison the following week.

Mrs. Gold and Mr. Harrison were in their eighties. They needed help from someone they could trust—someone who would not steal from them or lie to them. Becoming bonded was something a home helper could do. This was very important if they helped the elderly with their money.

Cecilia paid for her background check to be done. The police checked her records, and, of course, found nothing. She took insurance out on herself. If anything happened to a client's money, the insurance company would pay. Cecilia was honest and careful. She would never lose her clients' money. She would never steal it. Even so, being bonded and insured made her clients and their families feel better.

Cecilia put Mr. Harrison's banking papers into her car and locked it. Then she did some laundry. She changed the sheets on Mr. Harrison's bed. She asked Mr. Harrison about the medicine he needed from the drug store. "I'll pick up your pills after I go to the bank," she said. "I'll drop them off tomorrow morning." Then she drove to her last client for the day, sweet Mrs. Lee. Cecilia was behind. She needed to get to the bank, stop at the drug store, and get home to eat and change her clothes. Cecilia liked her night class in Lubbock, but it was a long drive. It made for a long day.

CHAPTER FIVE

Mrs. Lee lived on the bottom floor of an old two-story office building. Her father, Mr. Charles Wallace, had a hardware store in Sunflower in the 1940s. He sold tools, seeds, and parts to repair tractors and cars. In 1960, when he turned seventy, he closed his business. He turned the first floor of his building into two apartments. One was for him, and the other was for Mrs. Lee and her new husband, Andrew.

Mrs. Lee was an English teacher in the Sunflower High School. Andrew was a lawyer. The apartments were perfect for everyone in the family. The building was on the Sunflower County Courthouse square. If Andrew Lee needed to do any business at the courthouse, he could just walk across the street.

The county courthouse square was the busiest part of Sunflower. There were shops and a park. People could walk out the door and find anything they wanted. Hundreds of people came to the courthouse square on Saturdays from the farms and ranches around. They met and talked. They caught up and told each other news.

The Lees had three children over the years. Their grandfather Charles Wallace enjoyed living in the apartment next door. He spent a lot of time with his grandchildren.

In 1966, both Charles Wallace and Andrew Lee were killed in a car accident. They were driving from Lubbock back home to Sunflower. It was at night. No one could understand what happened.

Mrs. Lee told her friends, "I had a dream. A deer came onto the road. Andrew turned so he wouldn't hit it. Then they crashed." This caused a long silence. Mrs. Lee sometimes said things like that.

Mrs. Lee raised her three children by herself. Like most young people, her children left Sunflower after they were grown. One of her sons was a law professor at the university in Lubbock. His name was Andrew Lee, Jr. He was married to a professor at the same school. She taught business. They had two children, a girl and a boy.

Mrs. Lee still lived in the same apartment on the courthouse square. It was a beautiful apartment with large windows. Mrs. Lee had white lace curtains. She enjoyed looking out her windows at the courthouse square. They had large trees there and green grass. Although most of the businesses were now closed, and the buildings empty, the courthouse square was still a beautiful place. Mrs. Lee was happy there.

Once a week, her son came to visit from Lubbock. Sometimes he brought his young son and teenaged daughter. Andrew Lee Jr.'s wife never came. She was always too busy.

Two months ago, one of Mrs. Lee's friends had seen Mrs. Lee coming out of her apartment. Mrs. Lee seemed to be having trouble walking. She held onto the side of the building.

She moved very slowly. Mrs. Lee's friend got out of her car to help her back to her apartment.

"Mary," her friend said. "Are you OK?"

"I don't know," Mrs. Lee said, laughing. "I can't get my left leg to work!"

Mrs. Lee's friend called Andrew Lee, Jr. He drove to Sunflower right away. He took his mother to a hospital in Lubbock. The doctors said it was a small stroke. It was like an accident in her brain. It affected her left side. Her left leg and arm were a little weak. It made it little harder for her to walk, to lift things, or to dress herself.

Andrew, Jr. called Cecilia. He hired her to visit his mother six days a week. This was the hardest client for Cecilia in some ways. Six days a week was a hard schedule. Cecilia worried about Mrs. Lee. She was worried Mrs. Lee might fall. She thought Mrs. Lee needed more help than she could give for just a few hours per day.

CHAPTER SIX

Cecilia found Mrs. Lee sitting at the front window. She was looking out at the courthouse square. There wasn't anyone out today. Nabor's Drug Store was open. Cecilia could see a few cars and a truck parked in front of the store. The afternoon sun was bright.

Mrs. Lee said, "Cecilia, I think we're going to have a storm."

"Really?" Cecilia said. She pulled a chair over and sat down. "They didn't say anything on the TV news about rain."

Mrs. Lee looked at Cecilia and said, "Oh, we're getting a storm. I just don't think it will be the kind we usually get."

"Huh," Cecilia said. She thought about the many kinds of storms they got in West Texas. They got dust storms, thunderstorms with rain, thunderstorms without rain, ice storms, and snow storms. Under that, there was always the wind. She wondered which kind of storm Mrs. Lee meant.

Cecilia asked, "So... how are you doing today?"

"Oh, I'm fine. I made some breakfast. I'm getting a little hungry again," Mrs. Lee said. She was wearing gray slacks and a blue top. She had dressed herself this morning. It took a long time, but she did it. Cecilia had taught her how to sit on a chair to get dressed. This way, Mrs. Lee could keep her balance, and not fall.

"Well, let me see what you have in your refrigerator," Cecilia said. "There still should be some eggs, and some of that tasty bread I got in Lubbock. The one with the raisins?"

"My granddaughter Anita ate the bread," Mrs. Lee said.

"What?" Cecilia asked. "Did Andrew Jr. and Anita come over the weekend?"

"Yes," Mrs. Lee said. "Andrew Jr. told me he and his family are moving to Sunflower."

"What? Wow, that's great!" Cecilia said. She meant it. She thought Mrs. Lee needed her family close by. She might lose Mrs. Lee as a client, but she still thought it was a good thing. She asked, "Where are they going to live?"

"Well," Mrs. Lee said, "for a few weeks they're going to stay in the apartment my father lived in. Right next door. Then, they're going to move into the old Garcia house."

That explained the car and work truck in front of the Garcia house that morning, Cecilia thought.

"I'm glad to see that wonderful house getting fixed up," Mrs. Lee said. "I really liked Mr. and Mrs. Garcia. That house had the most beautiful kitchen."

"When do you think Andrew Jr. and his family are coming?" Cecilia asked.

Mrs. Lee answered, "This Friday. Do you know anyone who can clean up my dad's old apartment?"

Cecilia was out of the house cleaning business, but she thought Nancy Martinez wanted some cleaning work. Her son was starting university soon. Cecilia told Mrs. Lee she would ask Nancy to come over. Mrs. Lee could tell her what needed to be done.

The bread was gone, but Cecilia found some pasta. She boiled the pasta. She drained it and put it on a big plate. Then she added two raw eggs, a little butter, some cheese, and a little ham she found in the refrigerator. She tossed the hot pasta. The heat of the pasta cooked the eggs into a creamy sauce. She added some fresh green onions. She saw the recipe on TV over the weekend. It was a good way to get grains, protein, and vegetables into the same dish.

"Hmmm, that smells good!" Mrs. Lee said. "I can't eat all of that. You should join me for lunch." She looked at Cecilia with high school teacher's eyes.

Cecilia could not say no. They enjoyed the fresh hot pasta together.

Cecilia cleaned up. She made sure Mrs. Lee had fresh clothes for the morning. She made a shopping list for the grocery store.

"So you think we're going to have a storm?" Cecilia asked. "I have to drive to Lubbock tonight."

"Be careful then," Mrs. Lee said. She started to say something else but stopped.

"What is it?" Cecilia said.

"I saw a fire," Mrs. Lee said, "in my dream last night."

CHAPTER SEVEN

Cecilia was glad that she had the pasta at Mrs. Lee's house. She was running late. She needed to go home and change her clothes. She stopped at the drugstore for Mr. Harrison's pills. She drove over to Sunflower First Bank. She had banking to do for Mr. Harrison. The bank had a drive-in window, but Cecilia always went inside. She knew both of the bank clerks. She went to Claudia Miller with Mr. Harrison's deposits.

"Oh hey, Cecilia," Claudia said.

"Hi, Claudia. I've got some deposits for Mr. Harrison," Cecilia said.

"Right. This won't take long. Hold on," Claudia said. She handed the deposit slips back to Cecilia. Then she said, "Have you seen what's going on the Garcia house?"

"Yep. I saw a work truck there this morning," Cecilia said. "I sure was glad the Lees bought it. It's nice to see it fixed up again."

"Uh-huh," Claudia said. "It's going to be a really big job. New windows, new roof, new air conditioning, new heating. My cousin Jared is on the work crew."

"Good for him. Wow... it's been years since anyone lived in that house," Cecilia said.

Cecilia left to go home. She needed to go to her night class in Lubbock. Ten minutes later, she pulled under the tall trees in her front yard. She walked into her wide front door. She ran upstairs. She changed her clothes and put on fresh make-up. She made herself some strong coffee. She poured it into a Thermos to drink on the way home.

It would be late when she got back. Perhaps 11 or 11:30 PM? She turned on her porch light. It was bright now, but it wouldn't be at eleven tonight. She jumped into her car and drove to Lubbock.

The trip to Lubbock had two parts. The first part was a narrow two-lane country highway. Just south of Sunflower, the road went down into a small canyon. There was a very small river, and some tall trees with long grass that was green from the river. After a few minutes, the road went up again, out of the canyon. Then, it went straight south through flat, dry, empty country. The canyon was like a thin, green island in the middle of dry, brown West Texas.

Next, the road went through a small town that had a few empty houses and an empty store. Even the gas pumps were gone. The road was very dark. There weren't a lot of people driving on it. That part of the trip took forty minutes.

The second part of the trip was on a fast four-lane state highway. There were lights and there were towns. It was busy. From there, the drive into Lubbock took another fifty minutes.

Of the whole drive, Cecilia drove most slowly, and carefully, through the green canyon just south of Sunflower. There were lots of animals in the canyon. In the black night, deer, turkeys, or raccoons could cross the road. Cecilia didn't want to hit any animals with her car.

Once, many years ago, she tried turning on the radio when she was driving through the canyon. There was no signal. Not even KSNF 99.9 in Sunflower, and it was only four miles away. Over the years, Cecilia took that as a sign that she should just drive and be careful. Now, she even turned off her music CD during that part of the trip.

Today's drive was the same as any other day. Cecilia passed through the canyon, and then turned on her CD player. Tonight's CD was a group she didn't know, *Yo La Tengo*. There was a lot of guitar. She sometimes needed to listen to a CD twice to decide if she liked the music. After a while, the buildings of Lubbock appeared in the distance. The sun was starting to go down. Cecilia would be on time, but barely.

She pulled into the parking lot of the American Red Cross building and walked in. She carried her notebook, her pencils, and her Thermos of coffee. She wasn't done with her day yet.

CHAPTER EIGHT

The home healthcare night class started late. Their instructor, Ms. Cornelia Cheyne, wasn't at the whiteboard at the front of the room. Cornelia Cheyne was a nurse. She worked at a nursing home for the elderly in Lubbock. She also taught night classes for the American Red Cross on home healthcare.

Cecilia took a few minutes to talk to her classmates. There were 34 home healthcare workers in the class. They were all ages. There were both women and men. Some were taking care of older family members. Mrs. Varga, for instance, was taking care of her husband's mother.

Others were like Cecilia. They had small, one-person home healthcare services in small towns, like Ralls or Littlefield. Some worked for one of the big home healthcare companies in Lubbock or Plainview. As far as Cecilia could tell, the small services like hers cost less for the elderly and their families. The big companies cost more. The home healthcare workers who worked for them also made less money.

"Where is Cornelia?" Mrs. Varga asked. It was 6:15 PM—fifteen minutes late. Most of Cecilia's classmates were tired.

They had long days. They wanted to go home. At that moment, Ms. Cheyne walked in.

"Sorry I'm late everyone," she said. She wore her nurse's uniform. She had light brown hair, and a friendly smile. Tonight she looked tired, just like everyone else. "We have a few important things to talk about," she said. "But mostly I want to introduce you to a special guest."

She turned. A woman wearing a long-sleeved shirt and dark skirt came into the room. She moved without a sound. It was like she floated gently through the room. She stood next to Cornelia Cheyne. The class was completely quiet. The woman was of medium height. She was slender and maybe 45 years old. She had large, dark eyes, and a pale face. She gave a small smile and waited for Ms. Cheyne to speak.

No one knew what to say. The woman had a beautiful pale purple scarf over her head. You couldn't see her hair. *She was Muslim*, Cecilia thought.

She remembered a magazine article she read not along ago. When a Muslim woman wore a head scarf, it meant she was "covered." For many in the home healthcare class, this woman standing before them was the first covered Muslim they had ever seen. Cecilia had so many questions. *What was she doing here? How did she get to West Texas?*

"I have the pleasure to introduce Ms. Rana Barakat. She just completed her physician's assistant degree at the university hospital here in Lubbock. She is now a physician's assistant," Ms. Cheyne said. "Can anyone explain what a physician's assistant is?"

No one said anything. They were all still looking at Ms. Barakat.

Cecilia spoke up. "It's someone between a nurse, and a doctor? Something like that?"

"Yes," Ms. Cheyne said. "Ms. Barakat, can you say more?"

"Yes, thank you," Ms. Barakat said. She talked for a few minutes about her work. She could treat ordinary health problems, like big cuts and simple broken bones. She could do examinations. With a doctor's assistance, she could write prescriptions for medicine. She could order blood tests, or X-rays. She spoke English with a slight accent. She sounded a little British to Cecilia. She spoke formally. Instead of *it's* she said *it is*. Instead of saying *care plan* she said *plan for treatment*.

Rana Barakat was still talking. She said, "I work with the elderly. It is one of my specialties. Family health is my other area of specialty. Home healthcare workers have to take care of themselves, too. It is hard to take care of other people. This is why Ms. Cheyne asked me to speak with you tonight. I am going to guest teach. Tonight's first topic will be about hydration. This is about making sure our elderly clients get enough water to drink."

A few classmates nodded. They started taking notes. The class continued.

CHAPTER NINE

Finally, around nine o'clock, the night class ended. They talked about how much water the elderly needed to drink every day. Ms. Barakat called it *daily water intake* and *hydration*, in her formal, soft English.

Cecilia and her classmates learned how to look for signs that an old person was not getting enough water. For instance, they could press their fingers gently on a client's arm for five seconds. If their fingers left marks after a few seconds, then the person needed water.

To everyone's surprise, Ms. Barakat talked about home healthcare workers, and *their* health. Some of Cecilia's classmates laughed. But, some of them said, "Oh." It was true. Everyone was tired.

Ms. Barakat said, "Ms. Cheyne?"

Ms. Cornelia Cheyne started talking again. She talked about the need to eat well, including vegetables and three full meals a day. They needed to get enough sleep. She said that everyone needed at least one full day off per week. Everyone laughed at that. Cecilia made sure her Sundays were free. She turned off her phone. She wondered about Mrs. Varga. If she was taking care of a family member, how could she get a day off?

At the end of class, Cecilia's classmates stood up to go. A few of them talked outside the Red Cross building before they went to their cars. Cornelia Cheyne called Cecilia over.

"Cecilia! Ms. Hunter?" Cecilia turned around. Ms. Cheyne stood with Rana Barakat.

Cecilia said, "Thanks for the class tonight."

Ms. Barakat said, "You're quite welcome." She put out her hand. Cecilia shook it.

Cornelia Cheyne said, "I wanted you to meet Ms. Barakat. Now that she's finished her physician's assistant training, she'll be opening a medical clinic. In fact, she'll be opening a clinic in Sunflower."

Cecilia was surprised. She didn't know what to say. On the one hand, Sunflower really needed a doctor, but a physician's assistant would be fine, too. Having a medical professional in town would make Cecilia's job a lot easier. Right now, she had to take Mrs. Gold and Mr. Harrison to Plainview to see the doctor. Plainview was forty-five minutes away.

On the other hand, what would people think about a covered Muslim woman being their physician's assistant? There was the shocking event of 9/11. Several young men and women from Sunflower went to war in Afghanistan and Iraq because of it. One of them, Denny Miller, was killed. Cecilia knew Denny's mother, Claudia Miller, pretty well. She was her friend who worked at the Sunflower First Bank. Finally, Cecilia said, "Well that's exciting news. We need a clinic."

Cecilia talked to the two women for a few more minutes. She gave Ms. Barakat her phone number. She spent a few minutes standing by her car in the dark parking lot. To the east, in the direction of Sunflower, she saw a flash of lightning, and then another. In the flashes of lightning, Cecilia could see the outlines of huge clouds. They piled high into the sky. One thing Cecilia loved about her home was that you could see for miles. If there was a storm at night, sometimes you could see it forty miles away.

She left for the long, dark drive back to Sunflower. Her thoughts went on and on. She had so many questions. The home healthcare class was like that. She drank some coffee, and then a little more. She drove through the still darkness. The houses and towns were farther and farther apart. Soon, she was the only car on the road.

CHAPTER TEN

As Cecilia drove north on the small country two-lane highway, she saw the stars in the sky disappear. She drove into the storm she had seen from Lubbock. *Mrs. Lee was right*, thought Cecilia. She kept driving.

The wind picked up. Cecilia had a hard time driving straight ahead. A hard eastern wind was pushing her car to the left. Then suddenly, there was a bright flash of lightning ahead. For a split second, Cecilia saw the empty road far ahead in brilliant white light. *That was close!* she thought.

Another flash, and then the loud boom of thunder. A heavy rain started, and Cecilia slowed down. Then, she slowed down even more. She followed the narrow road as it went down, down, down into the canyon south of Sunflower. The rain came down even harder.

There was another bright white flash of lightning, just to Cecilia's right. She cried out in surprise. Another boom of thunder filled her ears. *What a storm!* thought Cecilia. *I'm right in the middle of it!*

The rain was coming down so hard that Cecilia could

barely see. She knew that she was on the road at the bottom of the canyon. The small river must be on her left. She knew of three or four large trees just up ahead. She felt like she ought to go to them.

She couldn't drive in this rain. She wanted to pull off the road, under the trees. She could rest in her car for a while until the storm moved away. Her car moved slowly ahead until she saw the trees. She pulled over and turned off the engine. For a long time, she heard only the hard rain. The wind pushed her car a little from side to side. The lightning moved off to the south. Except for the flashes of lightning, it was completely dark. Cecilia closed her eyes and waited.

It seemed like just a few minutes had passed. When Cecilia woke up, the rain had stopped. She sat up. She checked her car clock. It was nearly midnight. She must have been really tired. She had fallen asleep in her car.

The lightning was gone. It was safe to get out of her car. Cecilia opened her car door and got out to stretch. She took out the flashlight she kept in the car and turned it on. Except for the wind moving high in the trees, it was quiet. The storm was gone. The air had the beautiful smell of rain.

Cecilia used her flashlight to look around. Then she pointed it down at her feet. She wanted to see if she got any mud on her shoes before she got back into her car. Cecilia saw tracks in the rain-soft earth. They were long and curved. They looked like small parentheses around a very short sentence. They were the hoof tracks from a deer. It was probably still nearby. Cecilia may have scared it away when she woke up.

It was late. It was time to go home. Cecilia started her car. Then she drove up out of the canyon toward Sunflower and home.

When she got to her house, the porch light was off. Something must have happened to her Windspeed wind turbines, or to the electrical system in the house. Cecilia got out her flashlight again. She got inside her house. She found her electrical system box in the kitchen. She flipped a few switches, and her lights went on. Maybe the house was hit by lightning? It wasn't the first time. They had a lot of lightning storms in West Texas.

Cecilia was very tired. *I'll check the wind turbines in the morning*, she thought. She fell asleep.

CHAPTER ELEVEN

It was good that Cecilia made sure she had no client visits the next morning. That was the nice thing about working for herself. She could make her own schedule.

When she woke up, it was already eight o'clock. Cecilia almost never slept so late. Not even the morning after a night class. She could see a bit of sunshine. She wondered whether it was still cloudy from the storm the night before. When she looked outside, she saw clouds. It was strange not to have full, bright sunshine.

Over breakfast, Cecilia looked out her kitchen windows. One Windspeed wind turbine was turning, but the other two were not. That meant something happened to them during the storm.

Were they hit by lightning? Cecilia wondered. The wind turbines would shut down for two reasons. One was that they had been hit by lightning, which was not good. Cecilia might have to replace the machinery inside them. *Goodbye money!* she thought.

The other reason might be that the wind was very strong

during the storm. When that happened, the wind turbines automatically shut off. This stopped the machinery from burning up.

After a fast breakfast, Cecilia got dressed. She went outside in the cool air to look at her wind turbines. Her back yard was a little green. After a hot summer, her grass was brown and dry. If this rain kept up, she might see a little more green before winter.

Cecilia walked to the wind turbines. She opened a small box on one of them. She pressed a few buttons. She took a deep breath and waited. And slowly, very slowly, the big white blades of the wind turbine started to move. Cecilia looked up at them. She could hear their slow *whish whish whish* as the blades slowly cut through the air.

Great! she thought. It reminded her of the first time they were turned on. She had been with her father. The wind turbines had been his idea. Cecilia thought about that day. They had laughed from excitement. Cecilia thought that the words "mad scientist" described it. That day was one of the last things Cecilia and her father talked about before he died.

Cecilia left that good memory. She looked up. She saw that the wind turbine blades were going their usual fast *whish whish whish*. She went to the middle wind turbine and pressed the same buttons. She waited. The blades on this one started to turn.

Last night, the wind had been so strong that the wind turbines shut themselves off. That storm was worse than she thought. Perhaps when she was in the small canyon, under the trees during the storm, she hadn't felt it strongly. It had been very strong at her house.

Cecilia went inside to get ready for her day. She had to drive over to Mr. Harrison's house. She had his medicine in her bag. Then, she needed to call Mrs. Gold's doctor in Plainview. She wanted to make sure this Thursday at 10 AM was the right day and time to come. Last week she had driven Mrs. Gold all the way to Plainview, only to find the appointment had been cancelled. With Plainview so far away, it was a real bother.

What surprised Cecilia the most, though, was how unhappy it had made Mrs. Gold. She sat in the car. She was very quiet. Cecilia saw a tear run down Mrs. Gold's cheek.

Cecilia made a quick decision. The only thing that would help was a little shopping. There was nothing better for sadness than buying something pretty. It didn't have to be anything big or expensive. They went to the Plainview shopping center. Mrs. Gold bought a bottle of shampoo. Cecilia bought some fingernail polish called "Mexican Sunrise."

The "retail therapy" had saved the day. But, Cecilia still wanted to call the doctor this time to make sure they had an appointment that Thursday. She didn't want Mrs. Gold upset. Sometimes the elderly cared about things that surprised her.

Cecilia needed to spend a few hours with Mrs. Lee. If Mrs. Lee was feeling good, she would drive her to see the old Garcia house. She could see for herself what the workers were doing. It might bring back good memories of when the house was beautiful, and when people had parties there.

CHAPTER TWELVE

Cecilia dropped off Mr. Harrison's medicine. There was a lot of rain the night before at his house. He was outside looking at his rain gauge. A rain gauge was a clear plastic tube with measurements on the side. When it rained, the cup filled up, showing how much it had rained.

Mr. Harrison told Cecilia he measured almost half an inch of rain. "Maybe I can get my son Hack to plant some winter wheat," he said. "If we get more rain, my land will drink it up. I could get a good crop by May and sell it for a good price."

"Does Hack still know how to drive a tractor?" Cecilia asked. She laughed. She pictured Hack Harrison driving all the way from Dallas just to plant winter wheat, just because his 87-year old father asked him to.

"Oh yes," Mr. Harrison said. "He learned from an expert." He pointed his thumb at his own chest.

Cecilia then drove the twenty minutes to Sunflower. She parked on the courthouse square. She went into the office of the *Sunflower Reporter*. She wanted to know if they knew anything about the new medical clinic. Cecilia was thinking about it all morning. She wanted Sunflower to have a medical clinic. But, hearing just one person say it didn't mean it would really happen. She opened the office door. A small bell rang.

"Hey cat," Cecilia said, to the large black and white cat sleeping in the window. The sun had come out a little. The window was warm. The cat's ears and tail moved, but nothing else.

Jackie Neff, the owner of the newspaper, came out of the back. "Hey Cecilia!" she said.

"Hey, Jackie," Cecilia said. "How are you doing?"

Jackie's family had owned the newspaper for sixty-seven years. The two women talked for a few minutes about the storm and the old Garcia house.

Cecilia asked, "Have you heard anything about a medical clinic coming to Sunflower?"

"What?" Jackie said. She looked surprised. "I haven't heard a thing. Are you serious? We haven't had a doctor in town since 1995."

"Yep," Cecilia said. "I was at my home healthcare class last night in Lubbock."

"Uh-huh," Jackie said.

"I met a woman named Rana Barakat. She's a new physician's assistant. She said the university hospital wanted her to open a clinic in Sunflower."

Jackie grabbed a notebook and started writing. "Barakat?" she asked. "What kind of name is that?"

"Don't know," Cecilia said. She really didn't know. Ms. Barakat could be from any country, like Jordan, or Syria, or Iran. She could have been born in the United States. But, with her accent, Cecilia didn't think so.

Cecilia didn't tell Jackie her thoughts. Jackie could find out for herself. She was, after all, a newspaper reporter. Jackie might have only small-town things to write about. Things like high school sports, local dances, or farm news. But she was a good reporter. She found out things.

"I'll call someone I know at the university hospital," Jackie said. "I'll see what I can find out. We could use a medical clinic here in Sunflower."

"I hear you!" Cecilia said.

They spent a few more minutes talking about the storm. One ranch family near Cecilia had broken windows. A tree in their front yard fell down. Cecilia told Jackie about her two wind turbines stopping because of the wind.

It was time to go to Mrs. Lee's. As she walked to Mrs. Lee's building on the other side of the courtyard square, Cecilia remembered that Mrs. Lee didn't have any bread. She was getting hungry herself. She stopped by the Sunflower Pay Day Supermarket first. Maybe there was some chicken and salad vegetables. She could make some chicken sandwiches.

Mrs. Lee had talked about a chicken sandwich the week before. "I've just been thinking about cold chicken sandwiches for some reason," she said. "I've got a taste for them."

CHAPTER THIRTEEN

The Sunflower Pay Day Supermarket was only a few minutes away from the courthouse square. Cecilia walked. The sun came out a little more. There were still plenty of puffy silver and white clouds in the sky.

Cecilia bought some wheat bread, some chicken and lettuce, a few tomatoes and avocados, and a small jar of mayonnaise. When she reached Mrs. Lee's building, she saw Andrew Jr.'s car parked in front. She also saw Nancy Martinez's blue truck. Nancy must be cleaning up Charles Wallace's empty apartment. It might be ready in time for Andrew Jr.'s move from Lubbock on Friday.

Cecilia opened the door to Mrs. Lee's building. The door opened into a bright, sunlit hallway. The door on the right went to Mrs. Lee's apartment. The door on the left went to the apartment where Andrew Jr. and his family would live.

The door on the left was open. Nancy was inside with her sixteen-year old daughter, Luz. The windows were open. Fresh cool air came in. Nancy was in the kitchen, cleaning the sink and floors.

"Hi, Nancy! Nice to see you here," Cecilia said.

"Hey Cecilia!" Nancy said.

"Hi, Ms. Hunter," Luz said. She was a small girl, with short dark hair. She had a shy smile.

"It's nice to see you, Luz," Cecilia said. Then, to Nancy, she asked, "How's it going?"

"It's going," Nancy said. "Thanks for telling Mrs. Lee about me."

"Sure," Cecilia said.

Nancy said, "You know, I had no idea this great apartment was here! It's right across from the courthouse."

"You never know, do you?" Cecilia said. "I see these old buildings, and think they're empty and forgotten. They look like they're falling apart, but they're not."

She went to Mrs. Lee's apartment to make lunch. Inside, she found Mrs. Lee, Andrew Jr., his daughter Anita, his young son Jamie, and a thin blonde woman sitting in the living room. Young Jamie, a nine-year old boy, was standing next to Mrs. Lee, who was in her easy chair. He put a glass of water on the table next to her. Mrs. Lee said, "Thank you Jamie."

Andrew Jr. said, "Hey Cecilia!"

Up until then, everything looked fine. But then, Cecilia saw that everything else in the room was wrong. Mrs. Lee's granddaughter had long blond hair hanging down her back. She was medium-sized. She wore jeans and a "Lubbock High School" t-shirt. She didn't say a word. She just looked at Cecilia's orange "I Take Care of It" t-shirt and her red shoes, and laughed. It was not a nice laugh.

Anita looked like any high school girl. But somehow, something was off. She took up a lot of space. Her arms stretched out on the sofa, and her feet stuck out. She didn't move her feet when Cecilia walked past with the heavy grocery bags.

Andrew Jr., who was sitting on the other side of his mother said, "Anita." Anita pulled her feet in, but still didn't say anything. She took out her cell phone and started texting. Cecilia looked at her, then she looked at the woman, who was sitting next to Anita on the sofa. The woman was elegant. She wore an expensive gray dress. She had on a pearl necklace, and a heavy gold watch. She was working on a laptop. She didn't even look up when Cecilia walked in.

Cecilia took the bags of groceries into the kitchen. She expected to hear the family in the living room start talking to each other, but they didn't. Cecilia came out and stood next to Mrs. Lee. She asked, "Are you ready for lunch? Chicken sandwiches?"

Mrs. Lee didn't answer at first. Cecilia put her hand gently on Mrs. Lee's arm. Then Mrs. Lee looked at Cecilia and said, "Yes, that's good. I'll come and help you." She reached over to pick up her glass of water. Just as she did, Anita, the granddaughter, moved quickly and took the glass of water. She drank until the glass was empty. She watched Cecilia and Mrs. Lee as she drank. She put the glass back on the table and sat down again.

Andrew Jr. hadn't seen. He had moved over to the window with his son, Jamie. He was telling Jamie about the Sunflower County Courthouse. The woman on the sofa was still working on her laptop.

Cecilia had never seen anything like it. Mrs. Lee got very still. She picked up the empty glass. She followed Cecilia into the kitchen.

CHAPTER FOURTEEN

Andrew Jr. came into the kitchen. He kissed his mother on the cheek.

"Marcy is pretty busy with school things," he said. *Is Marcy the wife?* wondered Cecilia. Andrew Jr. looked unhappy. *Yes that's his wife,* thought Cecilia. *Oh dear.*

"If there's enough food, we'd like to eat with you all. I can help," Andrew Jr. said.

"Of course," Cecilia said. "We have enough for everyone. After lunch, I thought we could drive over to the old Garcia house."

"I'd like that," Mrs. Lee said.

Andrew Jr. said, "Sounds good. We can see how the workers over there are doing." Then he called out, "Jamie! Come on in the kitchen. Let's get some lunch started."

It turned out that Jamie liked to eat, and to cook. He said in his boy's voice, "You can't eat without someone doing the cooking first." Cecilia laughed. She got another glass of water for Mrs. Lee, and sat her down at the kitchen table.

Mrs. Lee told Cecilia how to boil water for the chicken.

"Put the chicken into the boiling water, and put the lid on. Then turn the heat off. Don't touch anything for twenty minutes! Then it should be perfect. We can cut it up for the sandwiches."

Andrew Jr. and Jamie washed the lettuce and tomatoes for the sandwiches. They cut up the avocados into slices. Cecilia took out the bread. She took out the toaster, and toasted the slices of bread. Mrs. Lee got up and took out six plates.

She worked slowly. She put mayonnaise on the toast. She and Jamie added the lettuce, tomatoes, and avocados, with salt and pepper. When the chicken was cool enough, Cecilia cut it into small, soft pieces. She piled the chicken onto the sandwiches and then put the sandwiches on the plates.

Andrew Jr. called out, "Lunch is on!" Silence from the living room. Then in a minute, Andrew Jr.'s wife, Marcy, came into the kitchen and sat down. Anita followed. "Sorry about that!" Marcy said. "I had to finish a little work." She looked at Cecilia and said, "You must be Cecilia. I've heard a lot about you. I'm Dr. Marcy Lee." She put out her hand. Cecilia shook it across the table.

"Nice to meet you. I'm Ms. Cecilia Hunter," she said. If Marcy was "Dr. Lee," then Cecilia would be "Ms. Hunter," not just "Cecilia."

Everyone ate without talking. The sandwiches were good. Cecilia asked how the moving plans were going. Marcy Lee answered, "Oh, fine. It's coming at such a busy time. But, we'll be here Friday."

"That's great. Everyone in town is real happy about the old Garcia house. It's great to have a family move *to* Sunflower for a change," Cecilia said. Anita laughed. Cecilia looked at her. Anita went back to eating. Then she picked up her phone. She started texting again, one-handed.

Now that Marcy Lee was off her laptop, she couldn't stop talking. She said, "I'd really like to see the high school while we're here today. Maybe we could talk to some of the teachers? Anita can't wait to get started. Right, Anita?" Anita didn't look up from her phone. Marcy Lee continued, "She'll miss her old high school, of course."

Anita continued texting.

After a silence, Cecilia said, "The elementary school is right next to the high school. Both schools are great. Really, they're the heart of Sunflower."

Marcy Lee looked at Cecilia.

"They're really important to the town," Cecilia said.

"Oh," said Marcy Lee.

Lunch was over. Cecilia got up to wash the dishes. Marcy Lee said, "Oh no, we'll do the dishes. It won't take long," She reached over and took Anita's phone away.

Anita decided it was time to speak. "Hey! Give that back!"

"Help me with the dishes first," Marcy said.

"That's *her* job," Anita said, looking at Cecilia.

"Get over here," Marcy said. Very slowly, Anita got up from the table. Somehow, Mrs. Lee's glass of water went crashing to the floor.

That girl is an accident, thought Cecilia. She wondered what her grandmother, Mrs. Lee, was thinking about.

CHAPTER FIFTEEN

Cecilia helped Mrs. Lee into her car. She made sure Mrs. Lee had her seatbelt on. Andrew Jr. and his family got into their own car. It took only a few minutes to get to the old houses on 6th Street.

There were two work trucks parked in front. The front door was open. Cecilia could hear the sounds of people working inside the house. She helped Mrs. Lee over the brown, dry grass. It would take a lot of work to make the yard beautiful again. This yard needed more than water.

Andrew Jr. led everyone into the house. Cecilia had never been inside. She could see that at one time, the house had been beautiful. Under all the dirt she could see old wood floors. They looked like hers at home. Her floors were honey gold, though, and clean and cool to walk on. Cecilia's house was built in 1927. She thought the old Garcia house was built at about the same time. The Garcia house had the same large windows. Now, new windows had been put in. They looked wonderful. "This is going to be a beautiful house," she said.

Marcy Lee said, "Thank you. I'm glad we bought it."

Cecilia thought, *I probably should start calling this the Lee house. It's not the old Garcia house any more.* Marcy Lee looked happy. Andrew Jr. looked happy, too. Cecilia could now better imagine they were married. It was nice to be wrong sometimes.

Mrs. Lee walked into the kitchen. It was being completely redone. There was a new refrigerator, a new stove and oven, and a new floor. Marcy Lee wanted to add an extra window. She went over to talk about it with one of the workers.

During the visit, Anita stayed outside. Jamie came inside with the rest of them.

Mrs. Lee told Cecilia she had seen enough. "It's going to be a beautiful home," she said. Cecilia thought so, too.

She called out to Andrew Jr. "I'm going to take your mother back home."

"All right!" he called from somewhere in the house.

When Cecilia and Mrs. Lee went out to the car, they couldn't see Anita anywhere.

"Cecilia," Mrs. Lee said. "Drive me to the high school, could you? It won't take more than five minutes."

"Of course," Cecilia said. She still had twenty minutes before she needed to drive to Mrs. Morris' house.

The streets of Sunflower were laid out in an interesting way. Of course, there was the Sunflower Courthouse square, which looked like a park. Everyone could see everyone else. People could walk anywhere they needed to.

Then there was 6th Street, filled with old homes. It went straight from one end of Sunflower to the other. At one end, was the old train station. No one used it now. There were no trains. It was still beautiful.

One half mile away, at the other end of 6th Street, was the Sunflower High School. You could look all the way from the train station, past the courthouse square, to the high school. Sunflower High School looked important. It looked large and strong. It was three stories high with large windows. It was made from light-colored brick. The double front doors were painted bright red. The front of the school was what every person in Sunflower thought about when they thought of home. Almost everyone in Sunflower had gone to school there.

Cecilia and Mrs. Lee parked in front of the high school. Cecilia turned off the engine. She felt Mrs. Lee wanted to say something. Mrs. Lee taught English at the high school for thirty years. Perhaps she would talk about her memories of that. But she didn't say anything. She just looked at the school.

"What is it, Mrs. Lee?" Cecilia asked, gently.

"I couldn't sleep last night," Mrs. Lee said. "Bad dreams."

"What dreams did you have?" Cecilia asked.

"Storms," Mrs. Lee said. "And fire. Change."

"Well, your family moving back to Sunflower is a big change. Perhaps you're excited about that," Cecilia said.

But Mrs. Lee didn't say anything more.

CHAPTER SIXTEEN

The rest of the week went by quickly. Cecilia visited Mr. Harrison once more. She helped him move his living room furniture around. He said he might move his bed downstairs. It was too hard to walk up to the second floor to sleep. The only bathroom was on the first floor of the house.

Next, Cecilia took Mrs. Gold to the doctor's in Plainview on Thursday. Essie Gold was fine. The doctor said she could stop taking one of her medicines. This was a good thing. As a treat, they stopped at a small barbecue restaurant. They had delicious barbecue beef sandwiches with potato salad and beans. Cecilia had asked for a green lettuce and tomato salad. The owner said they didn't have any. He pointed to the potato salad and beans and said, "Those are your vegetables! You don't need a salad to get your vegetables for the day!"

Cecilia laughed. Mrs. Gold said, "He's right, you know." Cecilia laughed even harder.

Each day, she visited Mrs. Lee. She seemed more relaxed. Perhaps she was sleeping better. Cecilia was there on Friday when Andrew Jr.'s family arrived with the moving truck.

Cecilia didn't stay after that. It was a big day for the Lee family. She thought they should enjoy it together.

There was another storm on Friday night, and another on Sunday night. They were gentle storms, with rain, and not much wind or lightning. Cecilia took the time to clean her own house. She did laundry and looked over her notes for her next home healthcare class Monday night. She took a phone call from a family who wanted her to take their elderly father, Mr. Percy Ellis, as a client. He lived in Ralls. He only needed one visit per week. Cecilia said she would schedule a home visit with Mr. Ellis. She wrote down his phone number. She said she would get back to the family by Wednesday.

That Sunday night, Cecilia went to bed early and fell asleep right away. She could hear thunder in the distance. It was another storm, passing to the south.

She began to dream. It was daytime, but she saw dark clouds piling up in the southern sky. Another storm was coming. She was in the small canyon south of town. She knew the river was on her left. Ahead she saw some trees. They looked smaller. She knew these were the same trees she had parked her car under during the big storm last week. She was not in her car, but walking. She walked faster. She knew that standing under trees might not be safe during a lightning storm. She wanted to go to the trees anyway. She felt that she needed to meet someone. She might be late.

In her dream, it got dark. The storm was coming quickly. Cecilia could smell rain. But she felt happy, because she saw two men standing under the trees. It wasn't far now. She could see the two men more clearly. One looked old, and the other was a man in his 30s. They both wore dark shoes and slacks, and light, short-sleeved shirts. The older man wore a dark, narrow tie. Cecilia had seen men's ties like that in old photos her father showed her. The older man smiled, and waved. The young man took off his glasses. He cleaned his glasses with a handkerchief. Then he put them back on.

Before Cecilia could get any closer, the storm arrived. A huge flash of lightning exploded right in front of her. A boom of thunder followed. It was so loud that Cecilia cried out. She covered her face with her hands.

When she uncovered her eyes, the men were gone. It was raining. But when Cecilia looked up into the trees where the men had stood, she saw a horrible sight. One of the trees was on fire! It had been struck by lightning.

Cecilia woke up. Her hands shook. She sat up. What an awful dream! She looked at her clock. It was 5:30 AM. She needed to get up anyway. She looked outside to the east, where the sky was getting light. There was no storm.

She jumped in her car. She had to see the canyon. She wanted to see if the trees had been struck by lightning. Cecilia got there within minutes. She parked her car under the trees. She spent twenty minutes looking at them from every side. She could see no signs of lightning or fire.

The trees looked very tall—taller than they had been in her dream. She had no idea what that meant. *Just a dream,* she thought.

Now she understood why Mrs. Lee had been so upset by her bad dreams.

CHAPTER SEVENTEEN

Monday was a long day, but Cecilia got to her home healthcare class on time that night. Ms. Rana Barakat was teaching. She told the class she was glad to see them again. She asked if there were any questions from last week.

One woman asked, "If I know a client needs more water, but she doesn't want to drink more water, what should I do?"

Ms. Barakat answered, "You could try adding a tiny amount of honey to the water. Or, try adding a small piece of cucumber to the water. Sometimes that is enough to make the water taste better."

Tonight's topic was watching for bruises on the elderly. Ms. Barakat told them that the black and blue marks on old people's arms or legs weren't unusual. They had thin skin. The elderly bruised easily. But, if an old person had many new bruises, a home healthcare person needed to find out why. For instance, an old person may have trouble standing or walking. They might fall. That would make new bruises. They might need to see a doctor about their balance. Or, fresh black and blue bruises might be a sign of abuse.

The word "abuse" made for a silence in the room. In her soft accent, Ms. Barakat said that anyone could abuse the elderly. If the abuser was a family member, an elderly person might not tell anyone about it.

One man in Cecilia's class said, "My brother sometimes dropped books and things on my dad. He made it sound like an accident. But then I saw bruises a third time. I knew it wasn't an accident. I called the police. It turns out he was asking Dad for money. Dad didn't have any money to give." There was a very long silence in the class.

"Thank you," Ms. Barakat said. She let a minute go by. No one said anything. Then she spoke again. "Sometimes the abuser can be a visitor, too. Perhaps someone in to repair a window. Or a friend. You must keep your eyes open. Bruises and black and blue marks might not be abuse. It might be a health problem. But, do not close your eyes to abuse. I can tell some of you are quite upset by the idea."

She ended the class with a short talk on recipes using fish. She also suggested adding beans to an elderly person's diet. Cecilia called out, "That won't be a problem. Go to any barbecue restaurant and they'll give you beans!" Everyone laughed.

After class, Cecilia spoke to Rana Barakat. Ms. Barakat thanked Cecilia for talking to the *Sunflower Reporter* about her. She talked on the telephone with Ms. Neff the day before for over an hour. "This will be a good way for the people in Sunflower to get to know me," she said.

"Sure thing," Cecilia said.

Ms. Barakat asked Cecilia if she knew of any place to rent in Sunflower. She planned to live in Sunflower.

Cecilia answered, "I might. Are you going to live by yourself?"

"No," Ms. Barakat answered. "My husband and our two sons will come. And, I hope, my father-in-law."

Hmmm, thought Cecilia. *It's going to be a big change for her family.* She said, "Have you lived in a really small town before?"

Rana Barakat said, "Yes, I grew up in one. Everyone knew everyone else. And everyone knew everyone else's business. Is Sunflower like that?"

Cecilia smiled. Ms. Barakat had it right about Sunflower, and about small-town life. Perhaps small towns were the same everywhere.

Cecilia said, "I may know of a place." She was thinking of Mrs. Lee's building. If Andrew Lee, Jr. and his family moved to their new house, old Mrs. Lee might want neighbors in the next-door apartment. She would ask her. Mrs. Lee might say no. But, she might say yes.

Cecilia made sure she had Ms. Barakat's phone number. She said she would call her sometime next week. Then she drove home. She thought about the night class, and how much she was learning. She thought about all the changes coming to Sunflower. As she drove slowly through the darkness of the small canyon near home, she saw nothing special. No storms, no fires, and no deer that she could see. There was just the gentle blackness of a warm West Texas night.

CHAPTER EIGHTEEN

The middle of October brought changes in the weather. Cecilia woke up one morning to a cold wind. It was the 21st of October. High clouds raced against the sky. She wore a sweater for the first time since April. By ten, it would be warm again, but at six, it was still cold. When Cecilia visited Mrs. Gold, Mr. Harrison, and Mrs. Lee today, she would check their house heating controls. If it got really cold, Cecilia had to make sure their homes would be warm enough.

Cecilia's first visit was to Mr. Harrison's place. Mr. Harrison's youngest son, Hack Harrison, had driven from Dallas the day before. Sure enough, he had gotten the tractor out. Cecilia found Hack's father sitting in back of his house to watch. Hack had gotten two large fields ready to plant. This morning, he was planting winter wheat.

After another hour, Hack finished and came to the house. Hack looked happy. Mr. Harrison looked happy, too. Cecilia had iced tea for them. Hack was certainly happy about that. October days were still warm in West Texas. The sun would be hot and bright until November or December. The winter wheat would need that to grow.

While his father was in another room, Hack talked to Cecilia. He asked, "Does Dad seem OK? His sleeping downstairs--is that normal? Should I be worried?"

Cecilia said, "No, don't worry about it. He just wants to be near the bathroom at night. Old people, especially older men, need the bathroom more often at night. It's just one of those things."

"Oh, OK," Hack said.

"You don't want him to fall down the stairs at night, right?" Cecilia said.

"Right," Hack said.

Mrs. Gold was having a bit of trouble drinking enough water. Earlier that week, Cecilia had pressed her fingers gently against Mrs. Gold's arm. She could see the shape of her fingers on Mrs. Gold's skin. Cecilia bought an orange at the store and cut it into slices. She put one slice into Mrs. Gold's water. She made sure the water was cold and fresh.

Sure enough, Mrs. Gold drank the whole glass. Cecilia suggested that she come three times a week, instead of twice. To Cecilia's surprise, Mrs. Gold said yes.

"All right, then," Mrs. Gold said in her high Texas twang. "That'll help me keep up with your fingernail polish changes!" Cecilia laughed. Then, after a short silence, Mrs. Gold said, "Just seems like with the colder weather I feel restless. I just want to keep standing up to look out my window. Like I want to fly away or something."

"Huh," Cecilia said. She wasn't surprised. When she saw the summer birds flying south, she felt like that, too. This morning, two large V's of geese and ducks had flown over her house.

Cecilia's last visit was to Mrs. Lee. Cecilia spoke to her about the apartment next door. She told her about Ms. Barakat. That she wanted to rent a place large enough for her family. "What an idea," Mrs. Lee said. "Let me think on that." It was 3:30 or so. Anita and Jamie were home from school. They were next door.

Cecilia and Mrs. Lee then heard a loud thump from Andrew Jr.'s apartment. Cecilia thought she could hear Jamie shouting... or was that crying? "What in the world?" she said.

She went out to the front hall. She knocked on the front door of the second apartment. Anita opened the door. Her long hair hung down her back. She had her phone in her hand. She looked at Cecilia. Her eyes were flat, like those of a fish or a cat.

Then she looked back at her phone. "What do you want?" she said, as she started texting.

"Hi to you too, Anita," Cecilia said. Anita didn't say anything. Cecilia gave up. "What's going on over here?" she asked. "Is your mom or dad here?" No answer. "We heard a thump and crying. Was that Jamie crying?" Still no answer. Just the sound of Anita's fingers on her phone. Cecilia was thinking about what to do next. Should she call Andrew Jr. or the police?

Then, Jamie came to the door. He moved fast around Anita and through the open door. Anita moved. Did she try to kick Jamie just now? He stood behind Cecilia. He said, "Mom and Dad aren't home yet."

"All right," Cecilia said. "You can wait with us." While she said this, Anita shut the door hard with a bang. Jamie and Cecilia stood in the sudden silence of the front hall.

"Let's go in to your grandma. You can tell us what happened," Cecilia said. Although she thought she knew.

CHAPTER NINETEEN

Cecilia was sorry about what happened next. When Andrew Jr. and Marcy got home from work in Lubbock, there was a fight. Marcy came in and found Jamie. Jamie had a black eye. Cecilia showed Marcy more bruises on Jamie's arms. While they put ice on his eye, Cecilia had seen a bruise on Jamie's hand. So, she gently asked Jamie to pull up his sleeves. He had black and blue marks all the way up his arms.

Mrs. Lee came over to hold Jamie. Jamie started to cry. *Was he ashamed?* Cecilia wondered. *Is that why he hadn't told anyone?*

Through the crying, Cecilia and Mrs. Lee understood: Yes, Anita had done it, three or four times. Sometimes she threw things at him. Other times, she just hit him. He didn't know why. She didn't yell. She just hit. The black eye was from a book she had thrown at him. The thump they heard was the book hitting the floor after it hit Jamie in the face.

Cecilia told Jamie's mother what Jamie had told her. Marcy went very white. Then she went back into her apartment.

Mrs. Lee, Cecilia, and Jamie listened as Andrew Jr. and Marcy Lee talked to their daughter. Then they shouted. Not a sound from Anita. *I hope they took her cell phone away*, thought Cecilia. *She might listen, then.* It was not Cecilia's business to see this kind of family trouble. But it *was* her business to look after Mrs. Lee. Mrs. Lee's safety was Cecilia's business. If Anita hurt Jamie, she could hurt Mrs. Lee, too. She would have to tell this to Andrew Jr. and Marcy Lee.

The fight seemed to end when Anita left the apartment. She slammed the front door. Things got very quiet after that. Cecilia had to go. It was dark, and she needed to go home and get ready for tomorrow's work day. She would talk to Andrew Jr. first thing tomorrow. Jamie probably needed to see a doctor. She would say that.

She asked Mrs. Lee to call her if she needed anything. "Anything at all. Any time," she said. "I mean it. I... I don't want you alone with Anita. Do you understand?"

Mrs. Lee looked sad. But her eyes were clear. She said, "I understand."

On the way home, Cecilia stopped at the *Sunflower Reporter*. She saw Jackie Neff's lights on. She might still be there. It got dark early in October. She walked in the front door. The little bell rang. This time, the black and white office cat was awake. He came over to be petted. "Ha! Awake, I see," Cecilia said.

Jackie came out. "Hey, my last customer of the day!" she said.

Cecilia bought a copy of this week's *Sunflower Reporter*. There was a front-page story about the new medical clinic coming to Sunflower. Cecilia read it while Jackie shut down her computers.

On page two, there was an interview with Ms. Rana Barakat, physician's assistant. Her picture looked good. She was wearing a head scarf. She had a warm smile. Underneath the picture there were details about her. Cecilia learned quite a bit. Rana came from Syria. She had been a nurse. She came to the U.S. in 2007. She had a scholarship to the physician's assistant program at the university hospital in Lubbock. She had family members here, but she also had family members in Syria. She was deeply worried about them. The war there was terrible. She was happy to start a life here in West Texas. She loved her work. She wanted to get to know the community of Sunflower.

Under the interview, there was an article that Jackie Neff had written. She told readers about the president's travel ban for travelers from many countries, including Syria. She gave a list of what she called "the questionable and poorly-thought-out points" of the travel ban.

"Ow!" Cecilia said. She was surprised. The cat had grabbed her leg in his mouth. He hadn't bitten her, but it still hurt. The cat was acting strangely. It ran back and forth in the front window. It meowed and meowed. Its tail stood straight up.

"Cecilia!" Jackie shouted. "Look! What is that?"

Cecilia looked out the front window. In the darkness, she saw an orange and red glow. The glow rose high in the sky. Fire! Then, she knew.

"Jackie, that's the high school. It's on fire!"

CHAPTER TWENTY

Jackie telephoned 9-1-1. The woman who answered the phone said they had the report. Fire trucks and police were on their way. Cecilia opened and closed her hands. Both Jackie and Cecilia were shaking. They had to do something. They both graduated from Sunflower High School.

The high school wasn't far away. They walked fast towards the fire. Cecilia could hear firetrucks in the distance. She could see police cars with their blue and red lights in front of the high school.

"Oh no! Look!" Jackie said. She pointed.

Cecilia saw fire shooting up out of the top floor. Cecilia and Jackie stood in front of the school. Soon, there were ten, then twenty, and then thirty people standing with them. They all lived in Sunflower. They heard the firetruck sirens and came to see the fire. They saw the horrible red orange glow.

Four fire trucks arrived. Two were from Sunflower and two came from Lockney, the nearest town. The firefighters went to work. They pulled out hoses. They turned the water on. They pointed streams of water at the top floors of the high school. The Sunflower Fire Chief spoke to the crowd of townspeople.

"You all know me," she said. She had to talk loudly to be heard. "I know you're worried about your school. Do not try to go inside. I know you're worried about the old photos in there, and other mementos of the school. Don't think about that right now."

"What can we do?" Jackie asked.

"Step back. We might need drinking water in a little while. Can anyone get some bottles of water?" the fire chief asked.

A few people ran to their cars. They would buy bottles of water at the Sunflower Pay Day Supermarket. If a firefighter or someone else needed a cold drink, the water would help. The rest of the townspeople just watched as their school burned. A terrible smell filled the air. It was the smell of fire.

After an hour, the firefighters beat the fire back. Now, there was just smoke. The entire third floor was burned. All the windows were broken. The beautiful light brick was black.

Suddenly, Cecilia's cell phone rang. She took it out. It was Mrs. Lee calling. She said to Jackie, "I've got to go!" She ran five minutes to her car. Then, she called Andrew Jr.'s cell phone. He answered. Cecilia said, "Your mother just called me. I'm a few minutes away."

"She did?" Andrew Jr. asked.

"Yes," Cecilia said. "Look, I know this sounds bad. But I want you to go over to her apartment. Check on her."

"Well, of course," Andrew Jr. said, and then he hung up.

When Cecilia arrived, she walked straight into Mrs. Lee's apartment. Mrs. Lee was sitting in her easy chair. She was looking at her granddaughter Anita. Anita was sitting on the sofa near Mrs. Lee. *What is Anita doing here?* thought Cecilia.

The idea of it made her feel cold. *Was Anita alone with Mrs. Lee, when Andrew Jr. came over to check?*

Cecilia looked over at Andrew Jr. He was standing in the doorway. He, too, was looking at Anita. *Were Marcy and Jamie in the other apartment?* Cecilia didn't know.

She asked, "Where's Jamie?"

Andrew Jr.'s answer was quiet. He said, "Marcy took him to the Lockney Hospital. It was the closest. She was worried about him." Then, he turned to Anita. "Anita, we're taking you to get help. Tonight. You really hurt your brother. That can't happen again. This is serious."

Anita didn't say anything. For once, she didn't have a cell phone in her hand. She just sat on the sofa. She looked at her father. She didn't look sad. She didn't look angry. She just looked.

Cecilia smelled something strange. She knew what it was. It was the terrible smell of the Sunflower High School fire. She thought the smell was coming from her. But then, she realized the smell was coming from Anita. Suddenly, she had a horrible thought. *Did Anita...?* She couldn't finish.

Mrs. Lee said, "Anita. You burned down the school. You started that fire. Then you came back into my apartment. To do what, Anita? Was my home next?"

Anita smiled.

CHAPTER TWENTY-ONE

Things became strange in the Lee home. Months later, Cecilia still remembered every minute. When she had bad dreams, she dreamed about that night. In her dreams, she saw the look of shock on Andrew Jr.'s face again and again.

"What fire?" Andrew Jr. asked. To answer, Cecilia opened Mrs. Lee's front curtains. Even this far away, you could see the flashing lights of the firetrucks and police cars. Cecilia said, "The top floor is gone. That smell is coming from her." She pointed at Anita. She said, "I didn't see you among the towns-people. Where were you?"

Anita stood up. Her smile was gone. Andrew Jr. moved to the door. "No you don't!" he said. "Stay right there." He started to call someone on his cell phone. Marcy? The police? He was having trouble. His hands shook. Anita pushed past him. She ran out into the night.

Two police officers stood outside. Whatever ideas she had about running were not going to work. Andrew Jr. and Cecilia watched as the police put Anita into the back of the police car. Andrew Jr. put a shaking hand to his face.

"Oh, my god," he said. He turned to Cecilia. "I know this is too much to ask. Can you stay here with Mother? I have to go to the police station."

Cecilia nodded. She went in to Mrs. Lee. They sat together for hours. Cecilia gave Mrs. Lee a glass of water to drink. She drank it. Cecilia got Mrs. Lee ready for bed. "It's late," she said. "You'll feel better if you get some sleep."

"I won't ever feel better," Mrs. Lee said. "That girl. That girl."

That girl, thought Cecilia.

Around one AM, Marcy Lee came home with Jamie. Andrew Jr. came a few minutes later. The three stood in the front hallway. They held each other. Cecilia couldn't watch. It was too hard. After a few minutes, Cecilia told the family she would be back tomorrow morning. She walked out into the night, to her car.

CHAPTER TWENTY-TWO

Cecilia slept in. Her eyes opened to bright sunshine. It was nine o'clock. When she went downstairs, she looked out her kitchen window. She saw her Windspeed wind turbines slowly turning. Behind the wind turbines, she saw thin black smoke in the distance. The high school fire was out, but some smoke still rose from the burned building.

Cecilia felt horrible. She could not think. This was strange for her. She was usually a woman of action. She always decided what to do. Then, she would make plans and carry them out. The high school fire was different. It was not something she could do anything about. She couldn't make any decisions about it—at least, not yet.

She could make decisions about her own life. She needed to change her schedule today. She was no good to anyone right now. Mr. Harrison's son, Hack, was still visiting. They didn't need her to visit today.

She started by calling Mr. Harrison. Next, she called Mrs. Gold, and then Mr. Percy Ellis. He lived all the way in Ralls, over twenty miles from Sunflower.

He told Cecilia, "Honey, we could see the fire all the way here in Ralls!" Cecilia heard that again and again over the week. People in other towns saw the glow from the fire. West Texas was very dark at night, you could see any fire, or any storm, from miles away.

In the end, Cecilia went on her daily visit to Mrs. Lee. She was worried about Mrs. Lee. She drove into Sunflower. She walked into Mrs. Lee's apartment. To her surprise, Mrs. Lee was up and dressed. She seemed fine. She said, "I want you to go with me to the Sunflower County Museum this morning."

"What?" Cecilia said. She was completely surprised.

"Yes. The walk will do us good," Mrs. Lee said. "We can walk and enjoy our good memories. There is no better place to do that than the county museum."

They walked the five minutes to the Sunflower County Museum. The elderly of Sunflower enjoyed going there. The museum had a large collection of photographs of Sunflower from the 1920s to the 1980s. Many townspeople went to see photos of their family members, friends, and schoolmates. Now, many of them were gone in the years past.

The museum had newspapers from seventy years ago. Mrs. Lee pulled out a large book called *The Sunflower Reporter, 1960 -1970*. After a few minutes, she found a newspaper article she wanted to show to Cecilia. It was dated 1966. The headline read: "Two Sunflower Leaders Die in Car Crash." It was written by John Neff, Jackie Neff's grandfather.

He wrote that the crash took place in the small canyon south of Sunflower. The men's car had flipped over. Cecilia looked at the photo in the article. It was very clear. She felt her heart go *thump thump thump*. Two men stood in the photo. One was older, and the other was younger. The younger man wore glasses. She had seen the two men before. She knew them. They were the two men in her dream.

Mrs. Lee said, "I always liked this photo of them. I took it at a picnic just a few days before…". She stopped. Then she said, "It was a good day. That's how I remember them."

CHAPTER TWENTY-THREE

Although Sunflower lost a high school, the town came back to life again. There were changes. The town improved. Over the next week, the townspeople learned how the police caught Anita. The newspapers and KSNF 99.9 radio never used her name. Fifteen-year-old children were never named, even when they did a serious crime, like burning down a school.

Anita had texted many of her friends in Lubbock the night of the fire. She told them she was going to burn down the school. *It's a stupid little school in a stupid little town,* she texted. Two of her friends told their parents. Their parents called the Sunflower Police.

At first, Anita said she hadn't done anything. Then, the police showed her the video from the security cameras at the school. The cameras' recorder was on the first floor. The first floor wasn't burned. The video clearly showed Anita putting a burning piece of paper into the garbage can in a third-floor classroom. They also found her cell phone. It was burned and melted, but it was hers. After she learned that, Anita stopped talking.

Anita was taken away. No one knew where. A month later, Cecilia read that she was given a four year prison sentence in a special prison for the young.

"Only four years?" Cecilia said to Jackie Neff. They were having lunch together. Linda's Café and Lunch Spot had opened the week before. It was crowded every day.

"Oh, I don't know," Jackie said. "My friend at the Department of Prisons says it may be longer than four years. If Anita does something wrong in prison, like hurt another person, she might have to serve more time. And, if they think she's crazy, they'll keep her even longer."

Cecilia wasn't too sure about that. Anita had hidden her true self well. Would others see Anita's lack of feeling? She felt cold when she remembered Anita's smile when her grandmother asked her about her plans. Cecilia was sure the Lee family would never be all right again.

But, over the next months, the Lee family surprised her. They surprised everyone. Rather than leave Sunflower, they moved ahead with their plans. Andrew Jr. and Marcy finished work on the old Garcia house and moved in. Jamie continued at the Sunflower Elementary School.

Marcy took a year off from her university. She spent time with Andrew Jr. and Jamie. She became a volunteer business teacher at Sunflower High School. She taught students how to handle money, and how to start a small business.

The school was ruined, so the classes were moved to two churches nearby. The next May, Sunflower High School had a graduating class of 23. The whole town went to the graduation, which was held at the Lockney High School. It was the only place big enough.

Mr. Harrison's winter wheat came on fine, tall and golden. It was harvested, also in May.

Ms. Rana Barakat came to Sunflower with her family. She opened the new Sunflower Medical Clinic. She and her family moved into Charles Wallace's apartment, next to Mrs. Lee. The Barakat family were the first Muslims to live in Sunflower County. One of Rana's sons was Jamie's classmate in Sunflower Elementary School.

There were sad moments, too. The state decided to tear down the burned school. It took ten days. When the old school was completely gone, Linda's Café and Lunch Spot had a special dinner for the high school teachers and their families. A month later, building on the new school started. It would be in the same spot.

Old Mrs. Gold died suddenly. Cecilia started visiting six days a week, but then, Mrs. Gold fell. She was making orange juice. She dropped an orange on the floor. While picking it up, she fell and couldn't get back up. It was too difficult for Cecilia to take care of her. Mrs. Gold had to go into a nursing home in Sunflower. Her 93-year-old sister from Dallas came to visit. Her own daughter had driven her.

That night, with her sister holding her hand, Mrs. Essie Gold died. Cecilia was there. She had a soft spot for the old woman—even her hair trouble and her love of fresh orange juice. Cecilia found herself putting away her orange "I Take Care of It" t-shirts. She ordered a new box of "I Take Care of It" work t-shirts in a sort of light purple.

Cecilia often thought about the terrible storm of last October. She wondered why she had stopped in the canyon. *Why had she parked under those tall trees, right at the height of the storm? Why there?* She'd never done that before.

She also wondered why Charles Wallace and Mrs. Lee's husband were in her dream. *Were they telling her something?* Maybe she had seen the old photograph of them before, and forgotten about it. Maybe she put that image into her dream. She didn't know.

She visited the small green canyon with its quiet little river and tall trees many more times in the months and years to come.

BOOKS IN THIS SERIES

American Chapters books by Greta Gorsuch

- *The Bee Creek Blues & Meridian*
- *Lights at Chickasaw Point & The Two Garcons*
- *Living at Trace*
- *Summer in Cimarron & Lunch at the Dixie Diner*
- *The Storm*
- *Cecilia's House & The Foraging Class*